The Client

Short & Steamy

By M.S. Parker

Table of Contents

Chapter 1

Sara

Central Park at five o'clock in the morning was my favorite time and place. New York was known as the city that never slept, but when running in the park so early, it was easy to pretend that I was the only one for miles.

I wasn't a native New Yorker, but I'd loved the city from the moment I moved here. It'd been six years now, and I'd never once considered going back to San Francisco. I'd only gone back to visit my uncle twice, but he never made me feel guilty. Uncle Takeshi was great that way. I missed him, but my life was here.

Skirting some rocks as I rounded a corner, I let my mind drift again. I'd run this particular circuit at least twice a week for the last three years, three times when the weather was good. I knew it by heart. It's one of the things I always loved about running. As my feet found their rhythm, I didn't have to think about things.

I'd always been one of those people who'd thought too much, analyzed everything, even when I was young. After my parents died, it got worse. I was only eight when it happened. Sometimes I wasn't even sure I really remembered them, or if what I thought were memories were actually a combination of pictures and stories. Uncle Takeshi had done his best to help me cope, and in the end, the only thing that worked was physical activity. I'd never played well with others, so instead of enrolling me in organized sports, he taught me martial arts. I'd joined track in junior high and found that running helped too.

It also directed me to the field of sports management. I graduated with my Masters from Columbia last year but hadn't been able to find a job in my field. While in college, I worked part-time as a yoga instructor. Now, I had an additional job that wasn't even close to what I wanted to do with my life.

I would've sighed if I hadn't been running. I didn't want to think about work, not when I had to be there in less than an hour. I just wanted to concentrate on the process of running, the simple physical exertion of it. Nothing complicated or emotional. Nothing that required decisions or contemplation.

I managed to fall into that rhythm, into that

place where nothing else existed but me and the path in front of me, the shoes on my feet. It was a beautiful morning in the middle of May, and I wanted to enjoy it. One of the things that losing my parents at such a young age taught me was to make the most of every moment.

Then, just as I rounded the next bend, the one that took me almost back to the beginning, I caught movement out of the corner of my eye. A tall, older man was in the grass doing what appeared to be tai chi, or something similar. Even as my brain was processing his movements, the man collapsed.

I didn't think twice as I veered off the path and headed straight for the man. As I went to my knees next to him, I pulled my phone out of my pocket and quickly dialed 911. I put it on speaker as I checked the man's vitals.

"This is 911, do you have an emergency?" A woman's voice came through just as I was trying to find a pulse.

"Yes," I said. I was out of breath, but calm. "I'm in Central Park and there's a man who just collapsed. He has no pulse and isn't breathing." Before she could ask, I continued, "I'm starting CPR."

"Where in the park are you located?" she asked.

I looked around as I began chest compressions, trying to find some sort of description to give the ambulance a reference point. I felt the cartilage beneath my palms crack as I shouted my relative location. The emergency operator was still talking, but I'd more or less tuned her out as the muscles in my arms started to burn. I knew what I was doing and I didn't need her to keep me calm. I wasn't exactly trained for this, but I didn't panic easily.

I lost track of time, aware only of the little physical things that told me minutes were ticking by. My shirt sticking to me, soaked with sweat. Losing all feeling in my arms but still forcing myself to continue chest compressions. The wind whipping my ponytail around to sting my cheeks.

And then I finally heard it. Ambulance sirens. When I raised my head to see how close they were, I saw that a small crowd had gathered. It was nice of them to have offered to help me.

Uncle Takeshi had also taught me the fine art of sarcasm, though that might have been unintentional.

"You're the one who found him?" A paramedic knelt on the other side of the body and held up his hands.

I sat back, heaving a sigh of relief as the paramedic took over compressions. I shook my arms, wincing as the blood flowed back into my fingers. Another paramedic approached and I pushed myself up to my feet. My knees popped and my legs almost buckled. I'd been so focused on how badly my arms were affected that I hadn't even felt the pain in my knees, or the way my feet had almost fallen asleep.

"Miss?"

I turned to see a police officer walking toward me. He glanced at the unconscious man who was now being transferred over to a gurney.

"Can I have a word with you?" he asked. I nodded and we stepped off to the side. "Your name, miss?"

"Sara Carr," I said. I ran my hand over my hair, suddenly overly aware of how sweaty and gross I must've been. I wasn't normally a self-conscious person, but this definitely wasn't a normal situation.

"Can you tell me what happened, Miss Carr?" the officer asked as he flipped open a notebook.

I nodded and told him everything, step by step. Then answered his questions as he asked them, even though I'd already explained everything. I didn't know why he bothered since it was pretty clear the guy had suffered a heart attack, but I wasn't about to tell the cops how to do their job. For all I knew, this was part of some on-going investigation.

By the time he was finally finished, however, I was starting to wish that I'd tried to hurry him along. I was going to be late for work, and that was even if I didn't go home and shower first. I was halfway to the bus stop when I realized I'd left my phone back in the park.

"Dammit," I muttered as I turned on my heel and started running. It was probably a long-shot that it was still there, but I had to take it. I didn't have the money to buy a new one.

Surprisingly, I found it right where I'd left it. Unfortunately, the battery was dead after my lengthy call to 911, which meant I couldn't call work to tell them I'd be even later than I'd originally anticipated.

I swore again as I climbed onto the bus. I ignored the looks I was getting from the other passengers and focused instead on my immediate plans. Going straight to work was my best bet. I could shower at the health club where I worked as a trainer, and I always kept a spare change of clothes. I could explain things, then, face-to-face.

Except it didn't work out that way.

The prestigious health club where I worked in Manhattan was known, not only for its discretion but also for the quality and appearance of its employees. And based on the looks thrown my way when I walked in, I knew I was in serious trouble.

"Sara, can I see you for a moment?" The manager, Chad, looked grim as he hurried me out of the room and into his office.

"I'm so sorry," I said. "I was on my run this morning and–"

"You're nearly ninety minutes late, Sara," Chad interrupted. When I opened my mouth to explain further, he didn't give me the chance. "And then you show up here looking like...*that*."

I fought back a scowl. He was seriously going to go there? Not exactly surprising, but disappointing nonetheless.

"A man had a heart attack in the park," I said. "I ended up doing CPR, then had to stay and give my account to the police."

Chad crossed his arms and raised his eyebrow. "That's your excuse? I think it's safe to say that you have a problem with your priorities."

Priorities? My hands curled into fists. Was he fucking kidding me? I saved a man's life, and my manager was going to lecture me about my *priorities*?

"I think we've known for a while that things weren't going to work out here," Chad continued.

"You mean since I told you to keep your hands off my ass?" I snapped back as my temper got the best of me.

Chad's face hardened. "That's enough. You're fired. Get your things from your locker and get out. I don't want to see you in here again."

I was too pissed off to argue, or even to threaten to go higher up with sexual harassment accusations. My day had been insane, and I hadn't even had breakfast yet. I'd had enough. I stormed out of the office, slamming the door behind me. Chad was still hiding when I emerged from the employee locker room, not that I expected to see him. He was a coward and everyone knew it.

I stepped outside and headed toward the subway. The bus wouldn't be back for another twenty minutes, but there was a subway station three blocks away. I didn't mind the extra walk. It'd burn off some of my excess energy before I got home, and maybe then I'd be calm enough to talk to Gordon about what to do next.

My fiancé, Gordon Cleaver, was also a trainer at the same health club, and he knew about Chad's previous flirtations. I hadn't wanted him to get in trouble for sticking up for me before, so I'd asked him not to say anything. If anyone was going to put their neck on the line, it'd be me. I refused to be one of those women who had men fighting her battles. I knew there were occasions when everyone needed help from someone else, but this wasn't it.

What I did need, however, was someone to talk things over with, figure out what my options were, and help me decide what the best choice would be. I needed a job, so I wasn't sure if taking action against the club for wrongful termination was smart. It would probably result in a few awkward conversations with potential future employers, and, ultimately, it was my word against his. The way I saw it, the only benefit to threatening a lawsuit was to get my job back. But I wasn't sure that was the best idea either. Chad was the sort of guy who held grudges, which meant working under him again would be a nightmare.

With all the thoughts and possibilities swirling in my mind, I was pretty much moving on autopilot. Up three flights of stairs even though the elevator was working. I'd gone into the apartment and was half-way across the living room before I realized that something was off.

Gordon wasn't sitting on the couch, watching the news like he usually did on his days off. But his shirt was on the floor.

And so were a pair of heels I didn't recognize.

My stomach clenched painfully. They could've belonged to his sister. Meghan sometimes came by to see Gordon, and she wore heels like that.

Except neither of them were in the main living space, and I couldn't figure out why they would've needed to be anywhere else.

Part of my brain screamed at me to leave. To go somewhere else for a little while, then come back later and pretend I'd never been here or seen what I'd seen. I could play ignorant, pretend that what my gut – and common sense – were telling me was wrong.

But I'd never been one to walk away from a confrontation, and if Gordon was doing what I knew he was doing, no way in hell would I stick my head in the sand and take it.

I squared my shoulders, took a slow breath, then let it out. I wasn't calm, but I was close enough to deal with this. My hands curled into fists as I got closer to the bedroom door. I heard them now, the unmistakable sounds of two people having sex.

I pushed open the door.

Okay, make that three people.

I stood in the doorway, frozen, unable to look away even though I really wanted to. Gordon was kneeling behind a curvy blonde, every thrust making her large breasts swing beneath her. Another man was sitting on a chair in the corner, stroking his dick while he watched.

He was the first one to see me. "Want to join us, sweetheart?" he said, his eyes sweeping down my body. "My wife likes to eat pussy while she's getting fucked."

Gordon turned toward me then, the color draining from his face as he froze. The woman didn't seem to care, pushing her ass back against him while he stared at me.

"Sara, I can explain."

I held up a hand. "Not interested."

"It's just fucking, babe," Gordon said, his voice close to a whine. He pulled out, earning a dirty look from the woman. "You know I love you."

His cock was sticking up, condom gleaming. At least, I thought, he had the decency to wear a rubber. My stomach churned.

"How many times?" I found myself asking. Then I shook my head. "Never mind. I don't want to know."

"I wanted to talk to you about it," Gordon said, rolling off the bed. "But you're so uptight when it comes to sex that I knew you wouldn't understand. This isn't cheating, and if you'd just give it a chance, you'd see that."

Anger cut through the hurt. "Don't you dare lay this on me," I said through gritted teeth. "If you wanted an open relationship, or you liked sharing partners...I'm not judging that. You should have told me when we first got together. *Talked* to me. That's why it's cheating, you asshole."

To my surprise, the guy in the corner stood, his expression serious. "She's right. If I would've known your girl didn't know about this, I wouldn't have agreed." He held out his hand to the woman on the bed.

"I'm not his girl," I said. I yanked my engagement ring off my finger and threw it at Gordon. "Not anymore."

"Sorry," the woman muttered as she and the man picked up their clothes and hurried away.

"I'm going for a walk, Gordon," I said, keeping my voice low and calm. "When I get back, you need to be gone. And I don't ever want to see you again, so make sure you get all of your shit, otherwise, it's going to the mission at St. Paul's."

"Sara–" he began and shut up when I thrust out a hand.

"In case you've forgotten, this is my apartment. Has been since before I met you." My nails bit into my palms. "You have the time it takes me to walk to the coffee place and back."

I turned and walked out, ignoring his pleas for me to wait, to let him explain. I didn't want to listen to him. I didn't want anything to do with him ever again. Just the thought of it made me sick.

Between Gordon and Chad, I wanted nothing to do with men in general for the foreseeable future.

Chapter 2

Dorian

Las Vegas was fun to visit, but I always enjoyed going home to the Big Apple. The hotels in the city of sin were amazing, and I never minded the attention that was thrown my way by admirers, but a part of me liked the anonymity that New York brought. While we scheduled some fights in other cities, all of the big matches were in Vegas, and when I was fighting, that had been even more true.

"Is there anything else I can get for you, Mr. Forbes?" The flight attendant gave me a polite smile.

Genevieve was pretty, but she was also married, which meant she was off-limits. I had no problem sleeping with employees, as long as they understood that it didn't come with job perks, but I never fooled around with anyone who was married – or engaged. Everything else was fair game though. And while I didn't always stick with one-night stands, I always made sure my partners knew that I didn't do relationships. No exclusivity. Not even the promise of another date. I was a few months shy of thirty, and I didn't have any plans to settle down anytime soon.

"I'm good, Gen." I smiled back at her. Sometimes it was nice having a woman around who I knew wouldn't hit on me. Someone I didn't have to pretend to flirt with just to satisfy her ego.

"I'll leave you two alone then," she said as she headed up to the front of the plane.

I looked over at the woman sitting across from me. Long legs, flawless complexion. Her hair was the color of honey, her tan clearly fake. Fake eyelashes too, and I was pretty sure her breasts weren't natural either. Might've even had some work done on her face, but she was gorgeous and that was enough.

Another reason I loved Vegas.

Showgirls.

Some guys liked strippers, but not me. I didn't see the point of paying women to take off their clothes when there were so many willing to do it for free. It wasn't arrogance that made me say it either. It was just a fact. I knew I was attractive, and I had money. Both things that tended to cause women to throw themselves at

14

me.

"Did you want anything to drink?" I asked.

Amber – or was it Anna – shook her head and uncrossed one long leg. She wasn't wearing her costume, but the dress she'd put on after the show didn't leave much to the imagination either. It wasn't sleazy, just clearly made to attract attention. Off-white, strapless and painted-on tight.

"You used to fight," she said, leaning forward just enough for her cleavage to push up just right. "I remember seeing your last match."

I was a bit surprised. Amber – that was it, I remembered now – must've been older than I first guessed. I hadn't fought in nearly six years, choosing instead to take over the family business. While I missed the rush at times, there was something to be said for keeping my face this pretty.

"I did," I said and shrugged off my jacket, loosening my tie.

After my business meeting, I'd taken several of the men I'd met to a show. They'd headed to a bar once the show was done, and I'd gone backstage to see if Amber would like a free trip to New York. We'd gone straight from there to the airport, so this was the first opportunity for me to get comfortable.

"How long do you think we'll have to keep our seatbelts on?" Amber asked, her voice

15

dripping pure sex.

I shrugged, my eyes narrowing as she ran her fingers over her breasts, then down her stomach. When she parted her legs, her already short skirt slid further up her thighs, and I could see that she wore nothing underneath.

I felt her watching me as she moved her hand under her skirt. She moaned when her fingers parted her folds, slipped over her clit and then inside her. Her fingers moved in and out, first one, then two of them.

"Let me see your tits," I growled, palming my cock through my pants.

She pulled down the top of her dress and a wave of lust washed over me. Her breasts were full and firm, her nipples a dusky rose and already hard. While one hand was busy between her legs, the other went to work on her breasts, squeezing and teasing her nipples.

The moment the captain announced that we could remove our seat belts, I had my cock out and was rolling a condom over it. I'd just finished when Amber was there, straddling my lap. She put one hand on my shoulder, reached down with the other to grasp my cock and hold it steady.

I moaned in appreciation as she sank down on me, her height putting her breasts right at my face. I leaned forward and ran my tongue across her nipple, then took it in my mouth and sucked, hard.

16

"Oh, yeah, baby," she breathed as she began to move. She rose up until just the tip was still inside, then drove herself down. Hard.

"Fuck!" I grabbed her hips and flipped us over so that she was on the seat.

Bending my head, I took her nipple between my teeth. She squealed, then screamed when I slammed into her. I took a moment to be glad she wasn't the first screamer I'd fucked during a flight, then concentrated on what I was doing.

She clawed at my back but didn't tell me to stop. If anything, she begged me to fuck her harder. I was just grateful I was still wearing a shirt. I liked some rough sex as much as the next guy, but I wasn't in the mood to be scratched up at the moment.

"Harder," she lifted her hips to meet my thrusts. "I'm close."

My phone rang and I raised my head. Amber glared at me as I reached for my jacket, but I ignored her. I wasn't about to miss what could be a business call, but I wouldn't stop what I was doing either. It wouldn't be the first time I'd talked on the phone while fucking.

"Quiet," I said as I rolled my hips. She moaned and I reached down to cover her mouth with one hand while I answered the phone with the other. "Hello?"

"Dorian?"

Shit. It wasn't someone about business.

"Jelani," I said evenly. "Is something wrong?"

Jelani Murrow was my personal trainer...and the woman I'd been seeing on-and-off for a little over a year. I'd been straightforward with her about the fact that we weren't in a relationship, but lately, I'd started to feel like she wanted more than I was willing to give her.

"I was just wondering when your flight was getting in."

Amber squirmed underneath me, and I looked down to see her pinching and twisting her nipples with one hand. Her other one was between her legs, fingers furiously working over her clit. Her teeth nipped at my palm, but I kept my hand over her mouth.

"It'll still be a few hours," I said.

I closed my eyes as Amber's pussy tightened around my cock. I couldn't quite hold back the strangled sound that rose from my throat.

"Are you okay?" Jelani asked.

"Fine," I ground out.

Amber's dark eyes shone up at me as her body moved against mine. She was a dancer, and now she was dancing underneath me, muscles tensing and relaxing, new kinds of friction rubbing in all the right places. I was vaguely aware that Jelani was still talking, but I wasn't paying much attention. All of my focus was on moving harder and faster, driving into Amber

18

until I finally found release.

"Yes!" Amber's head tilted back, my hand falling away in time for her cry to go unmuffled. Her body shuddered as she came.

"You bastard," Jelani snapped. "You're fucking someone, aren't you?"

"I don't do girlfriends, Jelani, you knew that." I was so close. I needed to get her off the phone so I could come.

"Fuck you, Dorian!" Her words were clipped, harsh. "I quit."

I tossed the phone onto the seat next to Amber and grabbed her hips. I needed to come. She squealed when I started to slam into her, but she didn't try to push me away, didn't ask me to stop, so I didn't. I kept driving into her even when she climaxed again, going over and over until, finally, I came too.

I squeezed my eyes closed and leaned over Amber, letting myself enjoy the rush of chemicals that flooded through me, the natural release of tension. I knew I'd need to deal with the ramifications of what happened with Jelani, but it didn't have to be now.

I pulled out of Amber and stood. With a grimace, I removed the condom and tossed it into a nearby trashcan. Protection was necessary, but that didn't mean I had to like the clean-up.

I yanked up my pants and fastened them, then walked over to the minibar. "Want anything?" I

19

glanced behind me to see Amber smiling.

"I think I'll take some champagne if you have any."

I poured her a glass, then poured my own Scotch. I pushed Jelani from my mind and turned back to Amber, studying her carefully. We had the rest of the flight ahead of us, and I thoroughly intended to enjoy every minute of it.

Chapter 3

Sara

I started out late on my run this morning, even for a Sunday. Usually on Sundays, I slept in until seven before heading out. Today, however, I hadn't even woken up until past eight.

The apartment wasn't too big, but I'd never lived here alone. When I was at Columbia, I'd lived in the dorm. Since Gordon and I had already been dating for six months by the time I graduated, it had made sense that when my college roommate decided to leave after just two months in our apartment, that Gordon move in. So I'd just gone from one roommate to another.

In fact, I realized suddenly, I hadn't had much alone time since I'd moved out here. Uncle Takeshi had done the best he could raising me, and we'd been a family of sorts, but I'd spent a lot of my childhood and teenage years in relative solitude. I'd never minded before, but now it felt weird.

Gordon's things were all gone by the time I'd gotten back from my walk on Friday. Well, that wasn't entirely accurate. He'd left all the shit that he should've thrown away. Razor blades and shampoo and all that. So I ended up spending yesterday cleaning the apartment. Now, there were no traces of the bastard left.

I was glad for that, because I didn't want to think about him anymore. I only wanted to be grateful that we hadn't started making plans for the wedding. I didn't even want to imagine how humiliating it would've been to explain that the wedding was off because I'd caught my fiancé with a pair of swingers.

I shook my head and pushed that thought out of my mind. I didn't want to remember what I'd seen. The problem was, the next thoughts that came weren't exactly good ones either. They were primarily concerned with how I was going to pay my upcoming rent with only what I brought in with my part-time yoga instruction. I would've barely had enough if I'd still been working at the health club. Now, I'd be lucky if I could afford to eat for the rest of the month.

At least it was a beautiful day and I had the rest of the day to myself. A run, then a hot bath. I was pretty sure I had a little bit of wine leftover from a dinner a few weeks ago. That, plus the last of the ice cream in the freezer and a good movie sounded like the best way to end the weekend. Tomorrow, I'd worry about everything else.

As I headed out of the park and down the sidewalk toward the subway entrance, however, I quickly realized that I had something new to worry about at the moment. At first, I hadn't thought anything of the limo parked at the sidewalk. There were always limos about in the city.

But then it started following me.

I thought it might've been a coincidence, but when I cut across the street, it came too.

Shit.

That was exactly what I needed right now. A rich stalker.

I began to jog. Fortunately, the streets weren't too crowded, and I was able to cut around and through. Except the limo was still following, and now I saw that there was a man following me too. He wasn't very tall, but he was bulky, and the way he moved told me he knew how to handle himself in a fight.

I was still a few blocks from the subway, but there were a lot of people around. However, I also knew that having people around didn't guarantee safety, especially when most people's eyes were glued to their phone.

Sneaking another quick look over my shoulder, I saw that the guy behind me was walking faster. I had two choices. I could either try to lose him, or fight. I didn't know how long he could run, but I imagined that's what he'd expect me to do.

So I'd do what I always did when someone thought they knew how I'd react or behave.

I did the exact opposite.

I waited until I was at a crosswalk and stopped with everyone else. I edged toward the closest building and waited for the man to come close enough. The moment he was, I reacted, reaching behind me to grab his wrist.

I felt his start of surprise but didn't give him time to react. I shifted, pulling him around in front of me where I quickly jabbed my fingers into his throat. He gagged, coughed, then stumbled as I swept my foot behind his. The limo was right there now and I threw the man against it, twisting his arm up behind his back.

"Why are you following me?" I demanded.

He looked over his shoulder at me. "Sara Carr?"

I glared at him. "What do you want?"

"Miss Carr?" A new voice came from the limo.

I leaned back to see the speaker without releasing my hold on the man pinned to the car. The guy inside the limo was gorgeous. Bronze-colored hair, chiseled cheekbones, and a pair of stunning violet-blue eyes.

But being good-looking didn't mean he wasn't

some sort of psycho.

"What?" I snapped.

He gave me a charming smile, like I wasn't considering breaking a man's hand. "My name is Dorian Forbes, and I'd like to offer you a job."

Chapter 4

Dorian

I'd done my research on Sara Carr so I knew who I was looking for. Long ebony hair. Dark brown eyes. Five feet, five inches tall, slender. Half-Japanese on her mother's side, she'd been raised in San Francisco by her maternal uncle. Graduated from Columbia with a Masters degree in sports management. Part-time employee at a health club and a yoga instructor.

I knew all of that. What I hadn't known or expected was for her to be a total badass. Or so beautiful. I'd seen pictures, but they hadn't done her justice.

When I'd gotten the call that my father was in the hospital, I'd feared the worst, and according to his doctor, if it hadn't been for the young woman who'd immediately started CPR, it probably would've been fatal. While Dad and I didn't always see eye-to-eye, particularly on my personal life, he was my father, and the only family I had left.

So I'd asked around and gotten the name of the woman who'd saved him. I'd considered going to her apartment to talk to her, but when the police officer I'd spoken with told me that Sara had been running in the park, I'd decided that I'd wait for her outside, approach her that way. I wanted to thank her, possibly offer her dinner or a gift of some kind.

I hadn't taken into consideration how it would look to have a limo follow her. When she started running, I sent Reggie after her, to let her know I just wanted to talk. And, clearly, that was an even worse idea. It had, however, given me the chance to see her in action.

The moment she'd slammed Reggie into the car, I knew I couldn't simply thank her and walk away. For the first time in a long time, I'd found someone who genuinely intrigued me.

I wasn't sure what it said about me that I found a woman taking down my bodyguard to be...well, hot. I wasn't after her for sex though. Jelani had followed through on her threat to quit as my trainer. I hadn't realized that she'd been that serious about me, though I supposed I should have. Our on-again, off-again thing had been more on when it came to her, and I'd been the one moving further away. Apparently, not far enough.

When I'd seen what Sara was capable of, and with her background, I'd impulsively decided to offer her a job. Then I spent the rest of yesterday wondering if I'd made the right call. I didn't usually do that, second-guess myself. I was the kind of man who stuck to my guns, who made smart decisions and trusted my gut.

And I didn't get nervous.

Ever.

Which was why I didn't understand the queasy feeling in my stomach or the way I'd been pacing around in my office for the past fifteen minutes. I technically had two offices, one at the official Forbes Fighting Corporation office downtown, and one here at the gym. The one at FFC was much bigger and fancier, but I still had a soft spot for the gym where I trained when I was a fighter.

I also thought it'd be interesting to meet Sara here rather than at my place where I had a small private gym set up for training. Plus, I figured she might not want to be alone with me until she realized I wasn't some crazy person who followed random women around offering them work.

When it was ten till seven, I headed out into the main area. Half a dozen guys were already warming up. We opened at four and didn't close until one since many fighters weren't able to live off what they made in the ring and had to work. I

28

was fortunate to be born into a wealthy family, so I'd been able to focus solely on training.

A couple of the trainers gave me nods or waves, but I was pleased to see that the fighters were all focused on what they were doing. That was good. I had no problem with people who only wanted to work out, but if someone wanted to be a fighter, they needed to be all in, which meant when they were here, they were here to train. No distractions.

When the doors up front opened, I started walking toward them, already expecting it to be her. It was, but she wasn't alone. Someone was holding the door open for her.

Tyrell Smoak was twenty-seven and in prime fighting condition. He was the FFC's best shot at a title and – without sounding arrogant – the best fighter we'd produced since me. At six and a half feet tall, he was three inches taller than me, and bulkier.

I was pretty sure I could still take him though.

I forced a smile and walked right up to where Tyrell and Sara were talking. She wasn't late, but I wanted to tell her that she shouldn't be talking on my dime. A stab of jealousy went through me. I couldn't deny that I missed that part of being a fighter. The way women would look at me, like they'd do anything for a look from me, a kiss.

"Miss Carr," I said with barely a glance in

Tyrell's direction. "I'll show you to the women's locker room. I reserved the main ring today, thought we might spar a bit. Feel each other out."

"Where's Jelani?" Tyrell asked, looking around.

I wanted to tell him that it was none of his damn business and that he needed to get his ass over to the bags and start his own work-out. I didn't do any of that though, because I genuinely liked the guy. Even if I didn't want him talking to Sara.

"She quit," I said. "Sara here is my new trainer."

"Is that right?" Tyrell said with his usual easy grin.

Sara glanced at the clock on the wall, then looked back at me, her eyes guarded. "I think I've got just enough time to get changed before it's time to start." She turned to Tyrell and offered him a smile. "It was nice to meet you."

"I'll see you around," he said and nodded at me. "Good to see you, Mr. Forbes."

As he walked away, I gestured for Sara to follow. When she went into the women's room, I went to the men's and changed out of my suit. I glanced in the mirror I passed on my way back out. Without my business attire, I looked younger, less like the CEO, and more like I had before, back when the only thing I'd had to worry about was a clean fight.

"Mr. Forbes." Sara was waiting just outside the door. "Let's take a couple minutes to warm up, and then we can spar."

I nodded in agreement and began to go through my usual warm-up routine. After a couple minutes, I glanced over at Sara and my dick twitched. Her clothes weren't particularly tight, but there was no denying the strength and grace in that body. She didn't have the full, lush curves I usually looked for in a woman, but there was something about her that made me wonder what she'd be like in bed.

She looked up just then and saw that I was staring at her. "Ready?" she asked, her pleasant tone making me realize she didn't know I'd been watching her.

I nodded and climbed into the ring. She followed, and I could feel eyes on us. I didn't look around, hoping the trainers would get the men back to work. I told myself it was because I wanted them to focus on what they were doing, and not because I didn't want anyone watching Sara.

"Ready?" I asked.

She nodded, taking a fairly casual stance. "Your move."

I came at her, intending to sweep her leg out from underneath her. Except she wasn't there. She'd spun around so that now she was at my back. She caught my arm and pulled it up behind me like she'd done to Reggie.

"I probably should've mentioned that I spent some time yesterday studying your old fights."

Well, damn.

I was impressed, but not so much so that I couldn't think to hook my foot behind me and around hers. She released my wrist as she fell, twisting so that she somehow managed to be on her feet before I'd turned around. Back and forth we went, blocking punches, trading kicks. It was like a dance, each of us testing, leading, reacting. I'd never felt so in sync with anyone before.

When I finally managed to get her pinned, I suddenly realized that I wanted to kiss her. Our bodies were pressed together, breathing fast, pulses racing. With all the chemicals rushing through my veins, it was no wonder I wanted her. Even knowing the physical reason for this immediate attraction didn't make me want her any less.

So I pushed myself up and off, then held out a hand to help her to her feet.

"Excellent," I said. "I think this is going to work out great."

"Good." She gave me a tight smile and walked off.

Right, I thought as I watched her – as I watched the other men watching her. This was going to work out just fine.

Chapter 5

Sara

My pulse was still racing faster than normal when I reached the locker room, but I chalked that up to the work-out I'd just gotten. I'd stayed in shape when I'd moved to the East Coast, but there was a huge difference between running and lifting some weights, and doing the sort of sparring that Dorian and I had just done. He was a former FFC champ who'd retired a few years back. I'd assumed that meant he'd been injured or had something medically wrong that prevented him from continuing to fight, but all the articles I'd found made it sound like he'd quit to take over running his family's company.

After the match we'd just had, I was glad I'd done my digging because I'd at least been semi-prepared for how good he was. What I hadn't been prepared for was how much I'd enjoyed the session. Part of me had relished the physical and mental activity that came with sparring rather than a workout, but I couldn't deny that I'd enjoyed it more than I ever had with Uncle Takeshi.

I wasn't a doctor or a nurse, but my area of study had focused on exercise and physical therapy, so I knew that vigorous physical activity produced vast amounts of chemical reactions and arousal wasn't an uncommon response. That tended to go up tenfold when the physical activity resulted in close contact with an attractive person.

Not that I was attracted to Dorian Forbes. But, I also couldn't deny that he was good looking. I wasn't blind.

"Sara!"

I turned when someone called my name. It wasn't Dorian, but someone I readily admitted was also attractive. I'd never been into UFC or MMA fighting, but once I'd figured out who Dorian was, I'd looked into the FFC. It hadn't taken me long to see that Tyrell was their newest poster boy.

"Aren't you supposed to be training?" I asked, sending a pointed look toward his annoyed-looking trainer.

He shrugged, his jade eyes sparkling. "Everyone needs a water break."

I raised an eyebrow, overly conscious of the eyes I could feel on me. I refused to give them the satisfaction of acknowledgment. I'd been around guys like this before. Pretty much every jock I'd ever met had looked at me the same way that the guys here were doing. It usually ended up being an odd mixture of condescension, annoyance and lust. None of which I appreciated.

Tyrell, at least, wasn't acting like I didn't belong here.

"I know you're not a fighter, at least not around here," he said. "But you know what you're doing."

"How do you know I'm not a fighter?" I asked, curious to hear his reasoning.

"Because I would've heard of someone as good as you," he said with an easy smile. "But you were using moves I've never seen before. Where'd you learn to do all that?"

"My uncle."

He took a step toward me, just enough that I could feel his body heat, but not so much that I felt like he was invading my personal space.

"Maybe you could teach me some of those moves sometimes."

My stomach clenched at the low tone in his voice, but I still played coy. "You'll at least have to buy me dinner first."

"I think I could manage that," he said, a dimple showing with his grin. "How about Friday evening? I'll finish up training around five, so I can pick you up at your place at six, or we can meet here at five-thirty, if that works better for you."

I had to give him some serious credit for giving me a choice. Not many guys would've taken into consideration that a woman might not want a virtual stranger knowing where she lived.

"I'll come here," I said and jerked my head toward his trainer. "Now get over there before Mr. Forbes decides to fire me and I have to start looking for yet another job."

Tyrell gave me another charming smile before trotting back over to his trainer. I let myself have a moment to appreciate the way his muscular body looked as he moved, how his ass flexed under his shorts. Then I turned and headed into the locker room.

I sighed as I stepped under the warm spray. One of the best things about a workout like the one I'd just experienced is that I could eat whatever I wanted and not have to worry about my weight. Which meant I'd be able to indulge in the steak, potatoes, and red wine I was craving.

I frowned. Or I would've been able to indulge if I'd actually been able to afford anything more than the cup of noodles I had sitting in my lone kitchen cabinet. I'd be able to get a few more groceries when I got paid, but definitely no steak, potatoes, or wine. Rent was a little more important.

Although, with as much as Dorian promised

to pay me – twice as much as my yoga classes did – I might be able to afford that meal in a couple weeks. Then again, with Tyrell taking me out on Friday, maybe I could get my steak that way. I definitely wasn't one of those women who thought I had to eat a salad in front of a guy. If I wanted a salad, I ate it. If I wanted meat, I ate it.

By the time I finished the shower and dressed, at least half of the men who were in the gym when I'd arrived were gone. Dorian was still there, and he'd clearly taken his own shower. For a moment, I couldn't look away. His hair was wet, and he was in a suit, looking like a strange combination of the man I met yesterday, and the man I sparred with just a short while ago.

I forced myself to look away before I could start having inappropriate thoughts about my boss. Then I saw who was sparring in the main ring, and let myself stare. I didn't know the name of the other guy, but it was clear he was no match for Tyrell. It wasn't a real fight, but I could see how good Tyrell was. Light on his feet, with a long reach and a way of putting all of his force behind his hits.

As I watched him, I couldn't help but wonder how all of that power translated into the bedroom. He was the sort of man who oozed sex appeal and confidence. The kind of combination that could either mean he awful in bed because he didn't bother to learn how to please his partner, or that he'd earned the right to that confidence because he was amazing in bed.

Maybe I'd be lucky enough to find out on Friday after our date.

Chapter 6

Dorian

I was starting to really dislike Tyrell.

Every morning for the past week, Sara came into the gym so we could spar and train. And every morning, after we were done, she'd stand around talking to Tyrell. I wanted to yell at him to get his ass back to training, but I knew if I busted his balls too much about her or insisted we change where we trained, the guys would start to wonder why I cared so much.

Hell, *I* wondered why I cared so much.

She was cute, I'd give her that, but it wasn't like I was hurting for sexual partners. I didn't need to be hitting on my trainer.

Okay, granted, I'd been fucking my previous trainer, but that wasn't the point. The point was, I hired her because she saved my father's life, kicked Reggie's ass, and I needed a new trainer. She piqued my curiosity.

That was all.

It didn't matter if I enjoyed the physical contact a bit more than I should have. I was used to having sex three, four times a week. I hadn't had it since the show girl the previous week. I'd been too busy with work.

At least that's what I kept telling myself. It certainly had nothing to do with the fact that I couldn't get Sara out of my mind.

Damn if I hadn't come just last night picturing Sara's lips around my cock.

"Dorian, you thinking about getting back into the ring?"

A voice from my left drew my attention away from where I was pretending to watch Chris and Jon spar. They were as good an excuse as any to keep my gaze in that direction.

"What was that, Paul?" I asked.

He grinned at me, flashing the three gold teeth he earned before retiring himself. "I asked if you were thinking about coming back to the ring."

"I like my face the way it is, thank you."

He shrugged. "Just thought that might be why you're coming in here every morning."

"Figured since I finally had a trainer who could challenge me, might as well enjoy it." I shot a glance toward Sara and Tyrell again.

"You think we could get her to fight for us?" Paul asked, following my gaze.

I shook my head before even considering the question. FFC mainly ran men's fights, but there were a couple up-and-comers who were starting to make a name for themselves in the women's leagues. While I didn't have anything against the idea of women fighting, I knew I'd never be able to watch Sara go through that.

"Better go get the boy back to work," Paul said. "It's gonna be hell getting him to focus the rest of the day."

It was an innocuous comment, but something about it made me tense. "What do you mean?"

I hoped it sounded as nonchalant as I wanted it to be.

Paul rolled his eyes and grinned at me. "Lover boy's got a date with your girl. Guess we know who's the champ after all."

I flipped him off, but I was only half-joking. I told myself that the knot in my stomach was because I didn't like the idea of anyone thinking Tyrell could've beaten me at my peak.

Except a part of me knew that wasn't the case at all.

I didn't like the idea of Tyrell and Sara going on a date, and I sure as hell didn't like the thought of them sleeping together.

I didn't want to sleep with her. Not at all. It was just that she was my trainer, better than Jelani had ever been. I didn't want some fling with Tyrell to fuck things up.

That's all there was to it.

And I kept telling myself that even as I tried to figure out a way to learn where Tyrell intended to take Sara tonight. I was just looking after her well-being.

When I decided I wanted to go out tonight, it had nothing to do with the fact that I knew Sara and Tyrell were out. When I chose to get pizza at Tribeca instead of one of the pricey restaurants where I usually dined, it wasn't because I knew that's where Sara would be. I was just in the mood for pizza. It happened...on occasion.

Once seated at the place with the best view of the restaurant, I perused the menu and pretended not to look for Sara.

I spotted Tyrell first, which wasn't a surprise considering how tall he was. He and Sara took a table directly in my line of sight but angled in such a way that, unless either one turned toward me, they wouldn't know I was there. Which was good, because I didn't want them thinking that I was following them.

Because I wasn't.

"Is that seat taken?"

I looked up at the woman I hadn't noticed approach. She was gorgeous. Tall, with long legs and great curves. A mass of blonde curls piled on the top of her head and big brown eyes.

"No," I answered honestly, then quickly added, "but I'm not looking for company this evening."

Her eyebrows went up and she stared at me for a moment, her hand still on the back of the chair she'd started to pull out. It was clear that she wasn't used to being refused.

"Sorry." I gave a half-hearted shrug as I apologized. I hadn't wanted to hurt her feelings, but I meant what I said. I didn't want company.

"Your loss," she said as she turned and walked away, putting a little extra swing into her hips to show me what I was missing.

I barely noticed. Instead, I was focusing on the way Sara had dressed for tonight. This wasn't a cheap pizza place, but it also wasn't some five-star restaurant where the food was more fancy than filling. The simple skirt and blouse was perfect first date material. Cute and a bit flirty, but not too revealing. Nice enough for something like this, but not so fancy that she couldn't have worn it to go to a club or ice skating, or whatever normal people did on dates.

Women I took out never dressed like that, first date or not, and we always went somewhere expensive. Because of who I was, they expected it, but I never minded paying because they always knew upfront that they wouldn't be around for long. I wanted sex without strings and they wanted to be seen with me. We both won.

When the waiter returned with my food, I was pleasantly surprised to find it delicious. Having been raised in a family who came from old money, I'd been taught that paying more for something made it innately better. While I'd never said out loud that I felt this way, I realized now that I'd been following that school of thought all along.

I frowned as I ate my pizza. I didn't like how that made me feel. I enjoyed having money, but I'd never considered myself a snob. Now, however, I was starting to think that I'd been mistaken all along.

Someone stepped into my line of sight. "Excuse me, aren't you Dorian Forbes?" A pretty redhead gave me a sweet, charming smile.

"I am." I leaned back slightly in my seat.

"I saw your last fight," she said. "You were so good. My brothers were all mad when you decided to retire."

"It's always nice to meet a fan." My smile was genuine, and I meant what I said, but hoped she'd move along so I could get back to...observing.

"My friend and I were wondering if we could buy you a drink." She motioned to her left and I looked over to see a petite brunette waving at us.

Last week, I would've had both girls naked in a hotel room within the hour. I wasn't the kind of man who was accustomed to threesomes, but I'd be lying if I said I hadn't had one before either. At the moment, however, the thought of these two women in my bed at the same time wasn't as appealing as it should have been.

"Thank you," I said. "But I'll be leaving shortly."

She looked disappointed as she left, but didn't press the subject, which I was grateful for. Tonight had ended up making me much more introspective than usual, and I tried to avoid that sort of thing at all cost. I didn't want to be thoughtful and kind. I enjoyed being shallow, enjoyed making the most of the pleasures in life and not giving a damn about anyone else. I wasn't cruel, but I always put myself first. I didn't know any other way to be.

I glanced at Sara and found her laughing. Even from a distance, I could tell there was no pretense in her. While she wasn't naive, she also wasn't fake. She made no apologies for who she was, and she behaved how she wanted, regardless of how it looked to those around her.

For me, there'd always been two types of women. The classy ones who occasionally slept with me after whatever function I escorted them to, and the ones like Jelani, who would never fit into my world. They were fun, great in bed, but that was all.

The women who moved in my social circles – the ones I took to events rather than just to bed – they knew exactly how they were supposed to behave, what they should say and what they should avoid.

Sara didn't fit either of those molds, and that confused the hell out of me. I liked things simple, but she complicated everything. I knew the smartest thing to do would be to walk out and never look back. Treat her as an employee only. Insist on training in ways that minimized the physical contact between us.

Forget about her and find someone for hot, sweaty sex.

That would be the smart thing to do.

Instead, I paid my bill and went straight home, unable to get the image of her out of my mind.

Chapter 7

Sara

The restaurant was amazing, the perfect combination of good food and a great atmosphere. It wasn't so fancy that I felt out of place, but it also wasn't the sort of cheap dive some guys would take a girl on a first date. Or, at least, my ex-fiancé wouldn't have gone for somewhere like this. Not that I was all about what a guy spent on me. In my opinion, it was the thought behind it that was important, and Gordon wasn't exactly the most thoughtful of men.

Tyrell, however, was a great guy. He'd opened the cab door for me, pulled out my chair, and hadn't once tried for any more physical contact than occasionally touching my hand. He was funny, sweet, and considerate.

I just couldn't figure out how in the world he was still single.

When the waiter put the pizza between us, I

closed my eyes and inhaled deeply, my stomach growling at the smell. When I opened my eyes, Tyrell was watching me. I shrugged. "I've been living off noodles and tap water the past couple days."

To my surprise, he laughed. Not a mean one, but the sort of sympathetic sound that said he completely got it.

"The year after I graduated college, I used to get down to ketchup sandwiches and lemon water."

I made a face and reached for a slice of pizza. "You went to college?" As soon as the words were out of my mouth, I regretted saying them. Heat suffused my face. "I'm so sorry, I didn't mean it like that."

He waved a hand and swallowed the bite he'd already taken. "Don't worry about it. I got what you meant. Most athletes in non-traditional sports don't go to college so they can participate in their sport as long as possible while they're still in their prime."

I gave a sigh of relief. That was exactly what I'd meant. "What'd you go for?"

He grinned at me. "Childhood education."

My eyebrows went up. "You want to be an elementary school teacher?"

Now there was a mental image. Tyrell towering over a bunch of little kids while he taught them their ABC's. Despite how ruthless I'd seen him be in the ring, I could picture him with children, helping them with math problems, making sure they all got their coats and boots on before recess. Somehow, it fit.

"I'm taking online Master's classes so when I'm done fighting, I'll just have to take the licensing tests."

My next bite of pizza halted mid-bite. "So you're already thinking toward retirement?"

I had to admit, it surprised me. Even I knew that Tyrell was something special in the ring. Pretty much everything I'd read in the past week said that he was on track to be even better than Dorian, and that was saying something. Barring serious injury, Tyrell had the opportunity to hold onto a championship title for at least half a dozen years. Even if he decided he wanted to go out on top, he could still be at it for a while.

Tyrell shrugged. "I enjoy fighting, and I'm good at it, but I don't live and breathe it, not like some other guys do. I want the title, but I'm not going to decide whether or not I want to keep it until I have it. I want more from life than that."

"Like teaching?"

"Teaching," he agreed. "And a family. Wife. Kids."

I arched an eyebrow. "Asking a bit much for a first date, don't you think?"

He grinned that wide, easy smile of his, the one that I knew melted the hearts of women everywhere. "Just laying my cards on the table."

There'd been a spark between us from the moment we met, and I was definitely attracted to him. I also wasn't entirely opposed to the idea of settling down, of marriage and a family. Having lost mine so young, I liked the idea of having a family of my own.

Hearing Tyrell say it like that didn't give me goosebumps, didn't make me want those things, but it didn't make me want to run away either. In fact, I didn't feel much of anything one way or the other. No jealousy at the thought of another woman having a family with Tyrell. No desire to have one myself.

I wasn't ready. No matter how much I liked Tyrell, no matter how attracted I was to him, I wasn't ready for a relationship.

He leaned forward and put his hand on mine. "Are you okay?"

I nodded, my smile feeling tight on my face. "I'm okay."

"But...?" He removed his hand and gave me a searching look. "Something changed, and I don't know what I did."

"You didn't do anything," I said, shaking my head. "I really like being here with you. You're a great guy."

"I'm hearing a 'but' in there somewhere."

Deep breath in. "Two weeks ago, I was engaged."

Tyrell's eyes darted toward my left hand, then back up to my face.

"Through a set of bizarre circumstances, I ended up getting home early and finding my fiancé involved in a threesome with a pair of swingers." There, I'd damned said it.

"Shit," he breathed, his eyes wide.

"Yeah, that was pretty much my reaction," I said dryly. "I knew things hadn't been going well lately, but I'd thought we'd just hit a rough patch." I stabbed an ice cube with my straw.

"I'm sorry," Tyrell said.

"I'm not." I lifted a shoulder and stabbed at the ice cube again. "I'm just glad I found out now instead of after I married the bastard." I looked up. "I'm not still in love with Gordon, but I don't think I'm ready for anything even close to serious."

"I understand," he said, his tone sincere.

I nodded, feeling more relief than anything else. I liked Tyrell. Liked flirting with him, talking to him. Hell, I even thought I might like sleeping with him. But I didn't want anything more than that. Not now, anyway.

I couldn't help but feel guilty as I opened my

front door. Tyrell had been so sweet and understanding. He'd accepted what I said, then continued on with our meal. We'd kept talking and joking, sharing stories about our past, our families. A part of me almost wished I was ready to date again. I had a feeling that a relationship with Tyrell would be easy, simple.

Completely unlike what I was feeling now.

All night, I'd been telling myself that the only reason I felt mild attraction toward Tyrell was because I wasn't ready to date so soon after my break up with Gordon. Except a part of me knew that wasn't entirely the case.

There was someone I was really attracted to, a man whose touch made my skin hum. Someone who I had a hard time not staring at whenever he was around. The man who'd been starring in my dreams almost every night.

If he asked me out, I wasn't sure I would give the same excuse to him that I had to Tyrell. In fact, I was almost certain that I'd have been looking forward to a second date – or maybe morning-after breakfast.

Just the thought of waking up next to *him* was enough to give me butterflies in my stomach, confirming my suspicions. I hadn't wanted to admit it, but while I'd enjoyed flirting with Tyrell, I hadn't gotten any of that same gut-clenching desire. Now that I thought about it, it'd been a while since I'd had that feeling at all. I could barely remember that fluttery feeling with Gordon. And I didn't even know if that was my imagination rather than memory.

I sighed and headed for the bathroom, shedding my clothes on the way. The food and company had been excellent. I just wished there could've been more. Tyrell was a great guy, and he deserved someone great too.

My thoughts didn't let up as I showered, or even after I climbed in bed. I attempted to read for a bit, but soon gave it up when I couldn't seem to make it past the same paragraph. I turned off the light and tried to sleep, but it was hours before I finally managed it.

My phone woke me up sometime before noon, but I just stared at it until it went to voicemail, watching Dorian's number fade to black. I didn't feel like talking to him on my day off, especially not after the thoughts I'd had last night. Just thinking about his voice made my entire body flush. I didn't know him very well, but I knew enough to know he wasn't the sort of man I wanted to get involved with, no matter how strong the attraction. Casual sex had never been my thing, and from what I'd heard around the gym, that was all Dorian did.

Not that he was even interested in me like that. We sparred well together, but that didn't mean anything.

Or maybe it did. I heard a couple of the guys

talking just the other day, saying that Dorian had slept with his previous trainer. I'd gotten the impression that some of the men were wondering how long it'd be until he did the same with me.

I sighed as I flopped over on my back and stared up at the ceiling. I knew I needed to check my voicemail and find out what Dorian wanted. We'd agreed to train five days a week, but also agreed that if we needed to change days around, we could do so. That was most likely why he'd called, and if he wanted to meet tomorrow, I needed to know it today.

I reached over and grabbed my phone, hitting the voicemail icon. My eyes widened as I listened.

He didn't want to change our schedule.

He wanted me to come to lunch tomorrow with his father.

Chapter 8

Dorian

I was starting to think this was a giant mistake.

Friday night, when I'd seen Sara out with Tyrell, I hadn't been able to stop thinking about her. I was usually pretty good at figuring people out, what they wanted, but I didn't get her. She wasn't like anyone I'd ever met before. The more time I spent with her, the more I wanted to know about her, know her.

And that's what I decided to do.

I needed to get her out of my head, which meant I needed to discover all I could about her so that I didn't find her so intriguing. Once she lost her mystery, I was sure I'd find her less attractive. Not that she wasn't pretty, but she wasn't really my type. Mystery was the only logical explanation for why she was constantly in my thoughts.

So if I solved the mystery, then my life could go back to normal. I'd be able to focus better at work, go out and find someone to hook up with. I'd keep her around for training since I hadn't felt so on-point since I'd quit fighting. I wasn't about to lose that.

“Will you quit pacing? You're driving me nuts.”

I looked over to where my father was sitting in his favorite armchair. He'd come home from the hospital just a few days after his heart-attack, and the doctors said he was doing well. For me, that meant he should be resting and regaining his strength. To him, however, it meant sitting around in his living room bossing me and his housekeeper around.

This was my childhood home, and like a lot of adults, coming back made me feel like time had rewound. I'd temporarily moved back in so Dad wouldn't be here alone, and while I loved my father, I was looking forward to getting back to my own place. To being an adult again. Aside from not having the privacy necessary to hook up with anyone here, having to listen to my dad talk about how much he wanted to meet the exotic young woman who saved his life didn't make it any easier to not think about her.

I told myself that I'd given in and invited Sara over because I was tired of listening to Dad complain, and it would keep him occupied for a while. The fact that it'd give me a chance to get to know Sara outside the gym was just a pleasant side-benefit. I wasn't trying to find ways for us to spend more time together. Just a part of unraveling the mystery.

"She said she was coming, right?" Dad asked.

I nodded as I crossed to the front window to check the driveway again. Our house was outside the city limits so I'd sent a car for Sara. It also made it easier to get to the house since our driver had the entry code. A part of me wished now that I'd driven into the city to get her. We would've had the whole drive to talk without interruption.

"This girl's got you in knots."

I didn't bother responding to his comment. I really hated how observant Dad was sometimes.

"They're here," I said as I saw the car round the bend. "Do you need any help to get to the dining room?" When he glared at me, I grinned. "Guess that's a no."

"That's a hell no." He pushed himself to his feet. "And we're not eating in the dining room. It's too damn formal. I had Martha set things up on the back porch. Bring the girl out there."

His tone was brusque, but I knew my father well enough to know that he didn't mean anything by it. That's just how he was. He liked to sound gruff, but he was the kind of man who'd give the shirt off his back to someone in need.

I headed for the front door, opening it just as

Sara was coming up the steps. I let myself have a moment to appreciate how good she looked. Dress slacks that showed off how long her legs really were, and a nice shirt that managed to be modest and flattering at once. A part of me was a little disappointed that she hadn't worn something flirtier, something more like what she'd worn on her date.

But this wasn't a date, I reminded myself. My dad had asked for it.

"Sara, thank you for coming." I kept my voice even, professional.

"Thank you for having me." She stepped past me and I caught a whiff of some sort of floral scent. She didn't wear it when we trained.

"My father's been quite eager to meet you," I said and gestured for her to follow. "It's all he's talked about since he came home, getting to meet the person who saved his life."

I was surprised to see a bit of a flush staining her cheeks.

"That embarrasses you?" I asked. "It's not like it's false praise. The doctors all said that if you hadn't done what you did, he wouldn't have made it."

I paused at the French doors that led outside. While I'd first met her with the intention of thanking her for what she'd done, I just now realized that I hadn't thanked her at all. Not really.

"It's been just my dad and me since I was five," I said, surprising myself with the admission. Surprised again as her dark brown eyes grew soft. "And I'm not an emotional person, but I can't deny that when I heard he was in the hospital, it scared me. So, thank you, for doing what you did."

Her eyes met mine, and for a moment, it felt like we were the only two people in the world. A few strands of hair had escaped the twist that captured the rest of it, and I had the sudden impulse to pull the ebony lengths from its confines, let it spill down over her shoulders. I wondered what it would look like spread out on my pillow.

I asked the question that had been on my mind all weekend. "Did you have a good time with Tyrell on Friday?"

Her eyes narrowed as she crossed her arms. "How did you know I was out with Tyrell?"

Shit. "I overheard some people talking about it at the gym." It was only a partial lie. I'd been trying to justify my interest to myself, but I doubted any of my arguments would hold water with Sara.

Fortunately, I didn't have to wait to see if she believed me or not.

"Stop keeping her for yourself, Dorian," my father called from outside.

I opened the door and held it for Sara, giving

her an exaggerated roll of my eyes. "Hold on, old man. We're coming."

Sara laughed softly as she walked over to my dad and held out her hand. "Mr. Forbes, it's a pleasure to meet you."

"Miss Carr, the pleasure is mine." He kissed the back of her hand and gave me a mischievous look over her shoulder. "And, please, call me Max. Mr. Forbes is my son."

I rolled my eyes. "She's too young for you, Dad."

"Says who?" He grinned.

Sara looked from him to me and back again. "You two are quite the pair, aren't you?"

I pulled out her chair before taking my usual seat across from my father. Martha had really outdone herself with lunch. There were cold cuts and homemade rolls, fruit, salad, cole slaw, and three different kinds of desserts.

Home cooking was definitely one of the things I miss the most about going back home. Take-out was generally my lunch fare...and dinner.

"Dorian tells me that you're from San Francisco," Dad began as he reached for a few apple slices.

"I am," she said. She made herself a ham sandwich as she continued, "I moved there after my parents died."

"I'm sorry to hear that."

"Thank you." She gave my dad a smile. "My uncle raised me after that."

"What brought you to New York then?"

It seemed like I wouldn't have to do anything except listen to get to know Sara if my father kept asking questions. When she finished with one, he brought up another. She answered easily enough, then fielded back her own questions. Though she directed everything to my father, I couldn't help but hope that her inquiries came from curiosity about me.

We stayed on the porch well after we'd finished eating. The weather was perfect and the view gorgeous. As much as there were things I enjoyed about living in the city, there was definitely something to be said for the tranquility that came from getting away from it all. When my father's health started to decline and he stepped down from running the company, I was surprised when he decided to live out here all the time rather than splitting time between the house and the city brownstone. I hadn't seen the appeal then, but now I could.

When I saw him starting to grow tired, I reluctantly cut into the conversation. As much as I wanted Sara to stay longer, I wouldn't risk my father's health to do it. I meant what I said to her, about how I felt when I heard about my dad's heart attack. I wasn't ready to lose him.

"You need to rest," I said as I stood. He

glared at me, but there wasn't any fire behind it. "Do I need to get Martha out here?"

"That's just playing dirty," he grumbled. He managed to get to his feet on his own, which was good because I knew he wouldn't be happy if I had to help him.

I picked up plates as he made his way to the door. Out of the corner of my eye, I caught Sara doing the same.

"I've got it," I said. "You don't need to do that." The glare she sent my way had me raising my eyebrows in surrender. "Follow me."

I led the way to the kitchen and set my dishes down on the counter. Sara was right behind me and did the same. Out in the hallway, I heard my father arguing with Martha about whether or not he needed to take a nap, but the sound was strangely distant.

"I suppose I should get going," Sara said, but she made no move to go.

My stomach twisted. I didn't want her to leave. I hadn't really gotten any alone time with her, and while I now knew a bit more about her history, I didn't know the things I wanted to know. What she liked. What she loved.

If she wanted to see Tyrell again.

"Do you have a date tonight?" I asked, trying to sound casual.

She shook her head, her eyes meeting mine again. "I don't think Tyrell and I are a very good match."

I resisted the urge to tell her that I agreed. Instead, I glanced at the clock. "Well, if you don't have plans for tonight, do you want to go into the gym and spar a bit? A couple of the guys are at matches, so it closed early. It'll be empty so we won't have to worry about spectators."

She studied me for a moment, and I wondered if those dark eyes could see through me, see what I didn't want to admit to myself, let alone her. If she did see it, it didn't seem to bother her.

"All right," she said. "Let's go. But if you think I'm going to take it easy on you because you fed me, think again."

"I wouldn't have it any other way," I said, trying not to stare at her ass as she turned to walk away.

I really hoped I knew what I was doing because this seemed to be heading nowhere good.

Chapter 9

Sara

I wasn't so sure this was a good idea. I'd enjoyed lunch more than I thought possible and had sincerely liked talking with Mr. Forbes – Max. I'd done my research on the family, so I already knew he hadn't come from money. That was his wife's legacy. Max's father had worked the floor in a plastics plant his whole life, and his mother had been a housewife. When Max married Dorian's mom, people assumed Max had only been after the money, but he'd proved them wrong when his investments and business ventures had led to an increase in the family fortune.

I'd known all of that, but what reading a bunch of articles online hadn't been able to tell me was that Maxwell Forbes was a down-to-earth guy who would've been just as much at home in a blue-collar bar as he was in the boardroom.

I'd actually been more comfortable talking to Max than with Dorian, but I could no longer deny why that was. Yesterday, I'd tried to downplay how much he had to do with why I hadn't wanted a second date with Tyrell, but the moment I'd seen Dorian standing in the doorway of his house, I'd felt with him what hadn't been there with Tyrell. Tension. Electricity.

Butterflies.

Dorian and I had barely talked the whole afternoon, only snippets of conversation that had included his father, but nothing had kept me from being hyper aware of his presence the entire time. When I'd followed him into the kitchen, it was like I could feel something connecting us, an almost palpable current. It wasn't unpleasant, but it did make me uncomfortable...mostly because I liked it.

When he asked if I wanted to go to the gym, I thought the physical activity would be good for me, burn off some excess energy, maybe ease some of the tension. Then again, sparring with Dorian was usually a good way to increase my tension rather than lessen it. When we moved together...I was all too aware of his body.

But I still agreed to go.

I wasn't ready for the day to be over yet either.

We talked a little on our way into the city,

mostly about unimportant things, the sort of mundane topics people talked about on first dates.

Except, I reminded myself, this wasn't a date. The lunch had been about me meeting Dorian's father. A gesture of appreciation for that morning in the park. That was it.

I took a couple extra minutes while changing to remind myself to be professional – despite the fact that I was now wearing a pair of yoga pants and a sports bra – and then headed out to the gym. Dorian was waiting, and as his eyes ran over me, I felt my nipples grow tight. My stomach clenched when I saw that he wasn't wearing a shirt, just a pair of shorts. His torso was defined, his shoulders broad above a narrow waist.

Shit.

I looked away from him. "Shall we?"

I took a slow breath as I climbed into the ring. I couldn't let him see my hands shaking. Too many questions I didn't want to answer. When I faced him again, I was composed.

We circled around each other, feeling for the best opening. He moved first and I countered. Then I moved and he countered. Round and round we went, feinting one way and then the other, blocking kicks and hits. We fell into our familiar dance; the same way we'd sparred during our first session.

But it didn't feel the same. It felt like...more.

This time, when I swung at Dorian, he caught my wrist and yanked me back against his chest. I sucked in a breath as his skin burned against mine.

"What's wrong?" he chuckled in my ear. "Didn't Tyrell teach you any fancy moves after your date the other night?"

I wasn't sure if it was the insinuation or the fact that I was so turned on that I couldn't think straight, but I twisted my wrist out of his grasp and swept my leg behind me. He thudded to the mat, a stunned expression on his face. Before he could get up, I was on him, my knees on either side of his waist. I grabbed his wrists and pinned his hands over his head.

I smiled down at him, pleased with myself for catching him off-guard. Then my eyes met his and any amusement I felt burned away. On most days, his irises looked blue, with just a hint of violet, but right now, they looked almost purple.

He worked his hand free, and I made no move to stop him. I couldn't. I'd heard of predators who mesmerized their prey, somehow made them stand still. I felt like that; like I was...spellbound.

He reached up and curled his hand around the back of my neck. For a beat, he held me there, as if considering something, and then he surged upward, his mouth catching mine in a fierce, bruising kiss.

I bit at his bottom lip and he parted my lips with his tongue. He sat up, one arm going around my waist as he held me against him. Our skin was slick with sweat, our pulses already racing, but the heat rushing through me had little to do with our previous exercise.

The smart thing to do would've been to end the kiss, get up and tell him that we weren't going to do this.

Except I really wanted to, and if what I could feel pressing against me was any indication, he really wanted to as well.

His hands moved to the straps of my bra, tugging them down my arms until my breasts were exposed. He wrapped my braid around his wrist, tugging my head back until he could kiss his way down my throat. I tried to run my hands over his chest, but my arms were restrained enough that I could only reach his stomach. The muscles there fluttered under my fingers, then jumped as my nails dug in when his mouth found my breasts.

I moaned as his tongue teased my nipples, and I ground myself down against him. He caught one sensitive piece of flesh between his teeth and I hissed.

"I want to fuck you," he growled the words. "Here. Now."

Bad idea.

Really bad idea.

"Yes," I groaned. "Yes."

Suddenly, we were moving, my bra straps sliding up so I could catch myself on my elbows even as he flipped me onto my knees. He yanked my pants and underwear down together.

"Fucking gorgeous," he muttered.

His hand ran over my ass, up my spine and then under me. He curled his body over mine, his cock hot and hard against my hip. He pressed his mouth against my ear even as he shoved my bra up over my breasts so he could cup them both.

"I've been dying to feel this body from the moment I saw you." He pinched my nipples between fingers and thumbs, chuckling when I gasped. "Now I'm going to make you scream."

I would've offered some smart-ass remark, but then his cock pressed against my entrance, and I didn't care what he claimed. I swore as he pushed inside, my body stretching to accommodate him even as I tried to spread my legs wider. My pants around my thighs kept me trapped, kept me impossibly tight even as he worked himself deeper.

My eyelids fluttered, fingernails digging into the mat. It'd only been a month since I last had sex, but Gordon's quick little wham-bam-thank-you-ma'am encounters the last few – okay, more than a few – times had felt nothing like this. I was barely aware of the sounds coming from

Dorian's mouth. The curse words. The moans. My name. All of that was in the background. Every bit of my focus was on the nearly overwhelming sensations coursing through each cell.

His fingers dug into my hips as he thrust into me, each stroke harder than the last, rubbing against all of the right spots until I was whimpering. My head fell forward and I squeezed my eyes closed. I was so close. I braced myself on one hand, moving the other one beneath me. I barely touched my clit and I came. Pleasure washed over me, through me.

"Fuck!"

Dorian stiffened behind me as he came, his hands gripping me so hard that I knew I'd have bruises in the morning. I didn't care though. All of the tension in my body had dissipated with my climax and I felt limp, relaxed. Even better, my head – which had been far too full recently – was pleasantly empty.

I knew it'd be full again shortly, and that I'd have to deal with what happened, but for right now, I was just going to take it.

Chapter 10

Dorian

I hadn't come that hard in a long time. My entire body was throbbing, pulsing. Sara's body was too. I felt her pussy spasm around me, squeezing almost to the point of pain. She was so hot and tight that it had taken an insane amount of control not to come immediately. I was surprised I managed to last as long as I did.

It wasn't until I pulled out that I realized how badly I'd screwed up.

"Fuck," I muttered.

"Wha..."

The word trailed off as the knowledge dawned on her face. The realization that we hadn't used a condom was quickly followed by the understanding that quite a bit of her was still exposed. Her entire body flushed and she yanked up her pants, then pulled down her bra.

"I'm on the pill," she said quickly, not

meeting my eyes. "And I always used a condom with Gordon, so I'm clean."

Shit! What the hell had I been thinking?!

I got to my feet and ran my hands through my hair as I turned away from her. Dammit! I was smarter than this.

"You'll excuse me if I don't just take your word for it." I felt the air between us shift, but I kept going. "I mean, no offense, but it's not like we actually know each other."

"You're right."

Her voice was cold, and something inside me twisted at the sound.

"We should both get tested as soon as possible. It's not like I know where your dick's been."

I turned, but she wasn't looking at me. Instead, she was climbing out of the ring.

"This doesn't count as a regular session." The words popped out of my mouth before I'd really thought about them. "I expect to see you here tomorrow morning, usual time."

"I'll be here."

There was no malice in her words. In fact, there wasn't anything at all.

"Thanks for the *sparring session*," she said as she reached the door. "It really cleared my head about some things."

I knew I'd fucked up before the door closed behind her, but it was too late.

And maybe that was a good thing.

I couldn't sleep, and it was seriously pissing me off.

The day had been going so well. Dad had finally met Sara, and they'd gotten along great. I finally felt like I was getting to know her, and then the heat between us when we'd sparred...

I hadn't been able to help myself when she was on top of me. I'd needed to know what her mouth tasted like, felt like. And things had just gone from there.

I couldn't stop thinking about her. What it was like inside her.

It'd felt so right, so natural. During the moments I was pumping in and out of her body, listening to her moans, feeling her skin against mine, I'd been able to put aside what all of it would mean, how what we were doing would change things. I'd been able to ignore how natural it felt, how much I'd wanted to take her home with me and spend the entire night exploring every inch of her body.

When we'd finished, and I realized that she'd made me lose control so badly that I hadn't remembered to use protection, it'd scared the hell out of me. I was always in control, even when I had sex. I was always aware, even in those moments when my body's natural instincts were taking over, I always held back.

Until tonight.

She'd made me lose control, lose myself. And for that, I'd lashed out at her in a way that made me sick when I thought about it. I could sometimes be a bastard when it came to women – okay, most of the time – but I'd never liked being intentionally cruel, especially not to someone who didn't deserve it.

Part of me wondered if she'd even show up tomorrow morning, or if I'd have to find yet another trainer. I was pretty sure I could get Jelani to come back. If I apologized well enough, things could even go back to the way they were.

But that's not what I wanted.

I didn't want Jelani training me and then sticking around for a quickie in the shower. I didn't want to call her some night when I was horny and didn't want to bother going out to a club to find some one-night stand. I didn't want to have to explain to her yet again why I wasn't going to be exclusive with her.

I knew what I didn't want, but couldn't let myself admit what it was that I *did* want. I told myself that I didn't know, but this was apparently one of those things that I couldn't lie to myself about.

Finally, after tossing and turning for hours, I decided to get up and go for a run. If nothing else, it'd clear my head before I went in to the gym. Usually, I would've gone to the park, but I didn't know if Sara still ran there. While the sheer size of the place meant that my chances of seeing her were slim, I didn't want to take that risk.

I also didn't want to risk running into my dad on my way out, so I crept down the backstairs and snuck out through the kitchen the same way I did when I was a kid.

The downtown office building where FFC had its official headquarters had a gym on the top floor so that employees of the various corporations could exercise on their lunch breaks. It'd been my dad's idea, and he footed the bill for most of it, but a good percentage of the people in the building took advantage of it. I generally didn't. If I wanted to work out in peace, I did so in my apartment. If I wanted a gym atmosphere, I went to the gym.

This morning, however, I went straight to the top of the building. A couple dozen laps around the indoor track were just what I needed. Once I got my head cleared, I could go to the gym, do a bit of training with Sara, and forget that last night ever happened.

I supposed it was a sound plan in theory. In practice, however, it didn't work out quite the way I wanted. I still had a bit of the usual endorphin high when I entered the gym, so things felt like they would work out perfectly. I nodded at the few guys who were already there and training, all the while scanning the room for Sara. She was usually early, and I was arriving right on time, so for once, she should've been waiting for me.

And she was...sort of.

She was here and dressed, standing near one of the bags in the back while she stretched. If that'd been all, I would've been fine, but it wasn't all because she wasn't alone.

Tyrell was standing with her, clearly staring at her ass as she bent to touch her toes. When she straightened, she smiled at him, the sort of coy smile that told me she'd moved right past what happened between us. Jealousy twisted dark and deep through me.

So much for everything going back to normal.

Chapter 11

Sara

No matter what I'd done, I hadn't been able to sleep last night. My brain kept running through the entire day, over and over. Everything from the moment I'd arrived at the Forbes' house, to how much I'd enjoyed spending time with Dorian and his father. And, of course, what we'd done after.

The memory of his hands and mouth on my body, how he felt inside me, all of it made me want him again. But then I'd remember the rest of what happened. The things he said, the way he behaved.

It had made me sick to my stomach, and I was still feeling nauseous the next morning when I headed to the gym. It was only sheer stubbornness on my part that made me go in. Not because I needed the money, but because I wanted to prove to Dorian that what happened meant no more to me than it had to him.

If only I could convince myself.

I didn't know what it was about Dorian that drew me to him, that had made me so completely forget myself, but I didn't like it. I wasn't a control freak, but I considered myself to be the sort of person who thought things through. I didn't behave impulsively. Or, at least, I didn't until I met him. I'd taken the job as his trainer without much thought, but I'd written that off as needing the money. I told myself that stopping things with Tyrell had been about needing space, but then I had sex with Dorian the very next night.

Unprotected sex. My gut churned and I reminded myself that I was already planning on getting tested right after work.

And then I was going to look for a better job, one where I didn't have to struggle to keep myself from either slapping or kissing my boss.

I showed up even earlier than usual, but mostly because I had too much nervous energy, and if I'd stayed in my apartment, I would've ended up pacing. Here, at least, I could stretch and warm up.

I'd only been stretching for a few minutes when Tyrell came over. I greeted him with a smile, and then immediately felt bad for the way his eyes lit up. I knew I didn't need to feel guilty though. I'd made it clear to him that I wasn't interested in pursuing a romantic relationship. If he read into me being polite, that was on him.

Out of the corner of my eye, I saw the front doors open and Dorian walk in. My stomach flipped, and I immediately bent down to touch my toes. I didn't want Dorian thinking I was looking for him. I could feel Tyrell's eyes on me, and wondered if Dorian was watching too.

"How are things looking for your fight?" I asked as I straightened. I was genuinely interested, but I couldn't deny that I was mostly asking because I needed something else to focus on instead of Dorian.

"Good," Tyrell said. "Paul says I'm in the best shape of my life. We're heading to Vegas tomorrow so I can adjust before the first fight."

I flipped my braid over my shoulder and smiled up at Tyrell. "That's great. I really hope you do well. You've worked hard and deserve it."

"Thanks." He ran his hand through his hair. "Listen, about the other night–"

"I'm sorry if I gave you the wrong impression," I jumped in, forcing my eyes to meet his. "It'd just been a long time since I'd gone on a date and I wasn't sure what I felt and–"

"It's okay." He reached out and took my hand. "I'd be lying if I said I wasn't disappointed, but it's okay. Sometimes great chemistry translates into romance, sometimes it's friendship." He squeezed my hand. "And that's what I'd like, if you're okay with it. Just because we don't work as a couple doesn't mean we can't still hang out."

Apparently, I was getting my signals all wrong. I thought Tyrell still wanted me, but now he was saying he'd be content with friendship. I thought Dorian had been interested in me as a person, but all he wanted was sex. I hadn't realized things with Gordon had gone so wrong until I caught him cheating.

I knew I was as much at fault for what happened between Dorian and me as Dorian, but I hadn't stopped to think about how last night wasn't the first time my judgement had been skewed. I'd written it all off as my attraction to Dorian, but now I wondered. Maybe that wasn't the case entirely.

Maybe I was just an idiot when it came to men.

I suddenly realized that Tyrell was still waiting for an answer. "I'd really like us to stay friends," I said. "My head's a total mess right now."

He smiled. "I get it."

Before either of us could say anything else, the sound of a door slamming caught our attention. Actually, it caught the attention of everyone in the entire gym. I saw the surprise on a few men's faces, but then they went back to what they'd been doing as if nothing happened.

"Well, Dorian's pissed about something," Tyrell said. He looked down at me. "I don't envy you having to train him when he's like that."

"Does he lose his temper often?" I asked.

Tyrell shook his head, a thoughtful expression on his face. "He's always been intense, but he never really snaps at people. It was one of the things that made him such a great fighter. He could focus all that intensity, but he never lost his temper and did something stupid."

Until last night.

But I didn't say that. I did, however, know that it was my fault, and I needed to fix it.

"Wish me luck," I said, hoping my voice sounded light.

"Luck," Tyrell said as I walked away.

I paused outside the door to Dorian's office and took a slow breath. I was pretty sure I looked outwardly calm, but my insides were still twisted into knots. I knocked.

"What?" Dorian barked.

I managed to not scowl. "I just wanted to let you know that I'm ready to start whenever you are."

Silence for a few seconds, then Dorian spoke again, "Go home."

I clenched my jaw, then forced myself to relax. "We can reschedule for later if you'd prefer."

"No." His voice was clipped. Cold. "I'm no

longer interested in what you have to offer."

I stared at the door, hurt and shock mingling with anger at his words. When he told me to come in this morning, I assumed that he would pretend like last night never happened. I'd been willing to accept that.

I sure as hell wasn't going to accept someone talking to me like that.

Spinning around, I headed for the door, feeling eyes on me as I went. But I didn't look at any of them, not even Tyrell. I didn't care about the clothes I'd left here or the fact that I needed the money this job provided. All I cared about was getting as far away from Dorian as possible.

I didn't even realize that someone was standing right outside the door when I pushed through, and even then, it took my brain several seconds to catch up to what I was seeing.

"Gordon?"

Coffee-colored hair. Blue eyes. Dimples.

It was him.

My cheating ex-fiancé.

"What do you want?" I snapped. I was aware that I didn't need to sound so sharp, but I wasn't in the mood to deal with anymore shit right now.

"I came to–"

The rest of his sentence was lost as someone grabbed my arm from behind and spun me around. I had a moment to register those near-purple eyes, and then Dorian's mouth was on mine, the kiss as fierce as the one we'd first shared last night. It was reckless need, the sort of thing that led people to do stupid things.

Like we'd done last night.

The memory was like a splash of cold water, and I pushed against his chest, the movement catching him off guard enough that I was able to break free. I took a step back, my shaking fingers curling into fists.

"Don't touch me." My voice was steadier than the rest of me. "You made your feelings about *what I have to offer* perfectly clear."

An arm went around my shoulders, and I smelled Gordon's familiar aftershave. A few weeks ago, I would've found it comforting, but now it made my stomach turn. Still, at the moment, it was better than staying here with Dorian.

"Come on, babe."

I let Gordon lead me to a cab, not looking back when I heard my name. I couldn't do this. I thought I could, but it was impossible to be around him. Not if he was going to be an ass one minute, then try to kiss me the next. At least with Gordon, I knew where I stood now.

I didn't listen to Gordon giving the cab driver an address, and I didn't look out the window when we pulled away just in case Dorian was still standing there. For the first minute or so, things were fine. Gordon stayed next to me but didn't say anything. I'd take a few minutes, get myself together, and then make sure the cabbie dropped me off at home before he took Gordon wherever he wanted to go.

I was still trying to clear my head when I felt Gordon's hand on my thigh. I resisted the urge to slap it away, but rather picked it up and put it back in his lap.

"Look, Gordon, I appreciate you helping me out back there, but I'd prefer if you kept your hands to yourself."

He scowled. "Come on, babe, don't be like that."

My eyebrows went up. Was he serious?

"I kept my distance to give you a chance to cool down."

"Cool down? This wasn't a fight over you leaving the toilet seat up. I caught you having sex with a woman while her husband watched. In my bed."

I felt the cab driver's eyes on us now.

"I told you that you shouldn't be so uptight about sex." He half-turned, his body effectively trapping mine against the door. He threw a glance over his shoulder, then smiled down at me.

A chill ran through me. I didn't like that smile.

He reached for me, one hand grabbing at my breast, the other going between my legs.

84

"Get off me!" I twisted, but there wasn't much room for me to maneuver. "Stop the car!"

"Keep going," Gordon ordered. "I'll give you something good to watch."

"Stop, Gordon!" I tried to shove at his hands, but I couldn't get him off me.

Suddenly, the car jerked, throwing us both off balance. I reached behind me, fingers scrabbling for the door handle. I heard the click a moment before the door gave and I was tumbling backwards.

I didn't try to stop myself, knowing that it would only jar my hands. Instead, I rolled into it, using the momentum to somersault backward and then push myself up on my feet. I didn't hesitate, didn't wait to see if he'd come after me. Instead, I just ran.

Chapter 12

Dorian

The moment I told her to leave, I regretted it, but by the time I got to my door, she was already stepping outside. I ran after her, not caring what anyone thought, only knowing that I needed to stop her before she disappeared. I had to make things right.

I knew I should've said something when I grabbed her arm, but no words would come. Instead, I did what I'd been thinking about all night.

I kissed her.

I hadn't even noticed the other guy until he was escorting her into a cab. Part of me said to take what happened as a sign that I really wasn't supposed to be with her, that she didn't want me. Except I felt it in her kiss. She wanted me. She was just pushing me away because I hurt her.

I wanted to make that better, to apologize.

I flagged down a cab and gestured in the direction the other cab had gone. I didn't know what I was going to say or do, only that I couldn't let things stand the way they were. We'd only gone a couple blocks when I saw the cab ahead of us jerk suddenly, then pull over to the curb. I was already reaching for the handle when the back door opened and Sara came tumbling out.

Shit.

Something was wrong.

I was out of the cab and running down the sidewalk before we'd even come to a complete stop. I heard the cabbie yelling after me, but I kept going. The man who'd been with Sara was out of his cab as well. She was running away from him, cutting through the crowd the same way she did when she was running from me that first day. The big guy was following, shoving rather than trying to move around people.

Adrenaline flooded through me and I followed him. My gut said that even though Sara had willingly gotten into the cab with him, whatever was happening now wasn't good.

She disappeared between two buildings, and the man was only a few steps behind. I put on an extra burst of speed, rounding the corner just in time to see the man shove Sara from behind. She tripped, stumbled, and fell, hitting the ground hard enough to make me wince.

Anger flared as I watched the man loom over

her. He was shouting something, but I couldn't hear the words. I did, however, see him draw his leg back to kick her, and that was enough to tell me that I wanted to beat the shit out of him. I didn't change my speed or direction, but I did shift my weight.

When I was just a few steps away, I shouted, "Hey, asshole!"

He turned exactly the way I'd predicted he would, and my fist connected with his jaw hard enough to make my arm go numb. He dropped like a stone, and I didn't need to look at him to know he was out cold. I'd always been able to tell when I had a KO.

Sara was already pushing herself up when I stopped next to her and stretched out my hand. Her eyes narrowed as she glared at me, but she took my hand and let me help her to her feet. Once she was up, my fingers tightened around hers.

"I'm sorry," I blurted out.

"I hope not for knocking Gordon out."

Gordon? This asshole was her ex? I scowled down at him and resisted the urge to kick him the way he'd been planning to kick her.

"No, I'm not sorry for that." I looked back at her. "I'm sorry for being such an ass. I was an idiot."

She gave me a hard look, then nodded. "Okay."

"Okay?" I repeated, surprised.

She looked around. "I really don't want to have this talk here."

I nodded this time, keeping her hand in mine as I walked us back out to the street. I caught the same cab, and when I gave the still-annoyed cabbie the address, she looked at me, surprised.

"Where are we going?" she asked warily.

"Where I should've taken you yesterday," I said, raising her hand to kiss her knuckles. "And where I'm going to apologize to you again."

"Would this apology happen to include orgasms?"

I choked on a laugh when I saw the driver jerk in his seat. "If you want it to."

"Are you going to be an ass again?"

"Probably," I answered honestly. "But I'll try really hard not to be."

She considered me for a moment. "If you ever treat me that way again, I'll knock your ass out."

I stared at her, knowing it wasn't even close to an idle threat.

"Now," she continued. "About those orgasms..."

89

Having Sara spread out, naked on my bed, was so much better than our frenzied fucking at the gym. Not to downplay how amazing it'd been, but this was better. Taking my time to explore every inch of her, knowing that once we were done, neither one of us would run away. Knowing that I could lie in bed with her all day and all night.

We had to talk at some point, work through some issues, but both of us wanted it, so I knew we'd be able to do it. For right now, however, my only focus was seeing how many times I could make her come.

I'd already given her one orgasm with my fingers, and I fully intended to give her at least one more with my mouth before sliding inside her. My cock was hard and throbbing already, but I ignored my own needs for the moment. I was eager to taste her.

She cried out the moment my tongue touched her, and I moved over her bare flesh slowly, teasing her, drawing out her pleasure until she was panting, writhing. I used my thumbs to hold her open as I dipped my tongue inside her, then slid it up to circle her swollen clit. She was so wet that she was dripping, and I moved my tongue over her, sometimes making long strokes with the flat of my tongue, sometimes tracing a path up and around her clit.

"Dorian!"

The sound of my name on her lips made my balls tighten. I'd always loved hearing women scream my name, but there was something special about hearing it from her.

"Come for me, Sara." I flicked my tongue against her clit, then pressed...hard.

Her fists thudded against the mattress, and she pushed her hips up against my mouth. I grabbed her hips, holding her in place as her climax rolled over her. I pushed her higher, further, until she was begging me to stop. Only then did I raise my head.

I'd fully intended to go down on her until she came for a third time, but I needed her too badly.

"Sara, can I...?" I let the question trail off as I raised myself over her.

She nodded, her eyes meeting mine. Her pupils were blown wide, irises nearly black. "Now," she rasped out, her voice rough.

Her arms went around me, nails digging into my back as I slid home in one smooth stroke. Her body molded around mine, the perfect fit. Some of it was probably biology, but I knew there was more to it than that. We hadn't known each other long, but there was something between us, something that couldn't be explained by logic or biology. It was a sense of completion, a sense of home.

I rocked against her, and she wrapped her legs around my waist. There were no hard thrusts, only slow, deep strokes, and when our eyes met, it was like I could feel everything she was feeling. The two of us moved together now like we did every time we sparred, more of a dance than anything else. My orgasm was building inside me, a slow sort of burn rather than the usual explosion.

"So close," she breathed, her nails digging into my back.

I nodded, not trusting myself to speak. I could feel her muscles quivering, feel her body taut with need. And then she was there, tipping over the edge, and I was falling too.

But I wasn't scared this time, because I knew she'd catch me, that I'd catch her. Nothing was perfect, and love was rarely easy, but I had no doubt that the two of us could make it.

I kept my body curled around hers as we came down and our breathing slowed. I brushed her hair away from her face and kissed her temple.

"You know," she said, breaking the silence. "It's a good thing you apologized."

"Oh really?" I asked, nuzzling her ear. "Why's that?"

"Because I'm pretty sure your dad was going to try to adopt me."

I chuckled. "Yeah, he really does like you." I pulled her closer. "But that's too bad. You're mine."

She sighed and closed her eyes. "Yes, I am. And you're mine."

Yes, I certainly was.

The End

Acknowledgement

First, I would like to thank all of my readers. Without you, my books would not exist. I truly appreciate each and every one of you.

A big "thanks" goes out to all the Facebook fans, street team, beta readers, and advanced reviewers. You are a HUGE part of the success of the series.

I have to thank my PA, Shannon Hunt. Without you my life would be a complete and utter mess. Also a big "thank you" goes out to my editor Lynette and my wonderful cover designer, Sinisa. You make my ideas and writing look so good.

About The Author

M. S. Parker is a USA Today Bestselling author and the author of the Erotic Romance series, Club Privè and Chasing Perfection.

Living in Las Vegas, she enjoys sitting by the pool with her laptop writing on her next spicy romance.

Growing up all she wanted to be was a dancer, actor or author. So far only the latter has come true but M. S. Parker hasn't retired her dancing shoes just yet. She is still waiting for the call for her to appear on Dancing With The Stars.

When M. S. isn't writing, she can usually be found reading– oops, scratch that! She is always writing.

Printed in Great Britain
by Amazon

22903816R00057